STAR WARS.

ADVENTURES

The Cavern of Screaming Skulls

GAME BOOK

STAR WARS®

ADVENTURES
GAME BOOK

The Cavern of
Screaming Skulls

Ryder Windham

SCHOLASTIC INC.

New York • Toronto • London • Auckland • Sydney
Mexico City • New Delhi • Hong Kong • Buenos Aires

ISBN 0-439-45907-9

12 11 10 9 8 7 6 5 4 3   3 4 5 6 7/0

Printed in the U.S.A.

First Scholastic printing, November 2002

YOUR ADVENTURE
BEGINS

For the full story behind your adventure, read up to page 48 in your Star Wars Adventures novel, *The Cavern of Screaming Skulls*. Or begin here.

You are a Jedi, the Skull Queen, or Klay Firewell. The *Adventure Guide* includes the rules for your Star Wars Adventures. You must follow these rules at all times.

You and your allies are in the fortress of the Skull Queen on Mount Octan, a volcanic mountain on the moon Nallastia. The Skull Queen's daughter, Princess Calvaria, has falsely accused the zoologists Tattyra and Hondu Firewell of being poachers, and has sentenced them to death. As a result, the Firewells are trapped in an energy field between three megaliths called the Trinity Stones. The magnetic attraction is causing the megaliths to slowly converge. Unless the energy field can be disrupted, the innocent zoologists will be crushed.

To save the Firewells, you must find and recover the Lost Stars of Nallastia, three legendary gems with auras that can shatter force fields. The Lost Stars are hidden on Mount Octan in the Cavern of Screaming Skulls. To travel to the cavern, you may choose from one of two vehicles: a battered swoop bike or a microweight. Faster than any speeder bike, the swoop is essentially a powerful engine pod with a seat and handlebar control. The microweight is an ultra-light repulsor vehicle, a glider with specially designed polymer wings. Both the swoop and the microweight can carry a single person.

After recovering the three gems, you must return to the Skull Queen's fortress and place one on top of each Trinity Stone. Only then will the energy field be disrupted and the zoologists be freed.

Choose your character. Each character has unique talents that are listed on his or her character card.

The Skull Queen and Klay Firewell cannot use Jedi Power, but they have their own power and talents (indicated on the back of their character cards). The Skull Queen is an expert tracker, and Klay Firewell is capable of handling dangerous animals. Compared with the Jedi, both the Skull Queen and Klay Firewell have a greater geographic knowledge of Nallastia.

Along with your one vehicle, you can take no more than three devices on this adventure. You can only use Power three times.

You start this adventure with your Adventure Point (AP) total from your previous adventure, or 1000 AP, if this is your first adventure.

May the Force be with you.

YOUR ADVENTURE:

THE CAVERN OF
SCREAMING SKULLS

Outside the fortress of the Skull Queen, you look at the forms of Tattyra and Hondu Firewell, hovering within the energy field between the three megaliths. The two zoologists appear to be frozen in time, suspended over the bones of poachers and other criminals, but you know the Firewells' time is running out. The magnetic power that binds the megaliths is drawing the three stones toward each other, making them close like the jaws of a vise. You must find the Lost Stars of Nallastia, the three power gems with the ability to disrupt energy fields, before the three megaliths meet.

According to legend, the power gems are located in the Cavern of Screaming Skulls. The entrance to the cavern is located on the northeastern face of Mount Octan, not far from the fortress.

You are one of five people who will go to the cavern and search for the power gems. The Nallastian V-wing shuttle has seating for only four, which means at least one member of your party must fly a one-person vehicle or ride standing in the shuttle.

To travel to the Cavern of Screaming Skulls, choose to either fly a one-person vehicle or ride in the V-wing shuttle. If you choose to ride in the V-wing shuttle, a one-person vehicle will be loaded into the shuttle's cargo hold in case you need it later.

To fly a one-person vehicle: Choose your vehicle. Roll the 20-dice to fly away from the fortress. Your roll# + your navigation# + your vehicle's speed# is your adventure#.

If your adventure# is equal to or more than 14, add the difference to your AP total. Your one-person vehicle lifts off and you fly alongside the V-wing shuttle, heading for the Cavern of Screaming Skulls. You may proceed.

If your adventure# is less than 14, subtract 6 from your AP total. Your one-person vehicle lifts you off the ground, but then the repulsorlift engine coughs and you start to drop back down. To restart your repulsorlift in midair, roll the 20-dice again. Your new roll# + your skill# is your new adventure#.

If your new adventure# is equal to or more than 12, add the difference to your AP total. The repulsorlift engine catches, and you soar up from the ground and fly alongside the V-wing shuttle. You may proceed.

If your new adventure# is less than 12, subtract the difference from your AP total. You restart the engine just in time to avoid crashing into the ground, but then the engine coughs again, and you can't restart it. Another one-person vehicle has been placed in the cargo hold of the V-wing shuttle, but you do not want to risk delaying your departure any longer. Proceed to ride in the V-wing shuttle (below).

To ride in the V-wing shuttle: Roll the 10-dice to sit back and ride away from the fortress compound. Your roll# is your adventure#.

If your adventure# is equal to or more than 5, add the difference to your AP total. The shuttle lifts off and cruises over the trees of Mount Octan, heading for the Cavern of Screaming Skulls. From the cockpit, one of your allies asks if you would like to take over the controls. You accept. You may proceed.

If your adventure# is less than 5, subtract the difference from your AP total. From the cockpit, one of your allies is having trouble with the navigational controls and asks you to take over. To pilot the shuttle, roll the 10-dice again. Your new roll# + your navigation# + your skill# is your new adventure#.

If your new adventure# is equal to or more than 8, add the difference to your AP total. With you at the controls, the shuttle handles with ease. You may proceed.

If your new adventure# is less than 8, subtract the difference from your AP total. Not entirely familiar with the shuttle's controls, you almost accidently send the vehicle into a steep dive. Go back "To pilot the shuttle," and repeat. When you have the shuttle under control, you may proceed.

As you fly toward the Cavern of Screaming Skulls, you encounter a flock of winged reptiles that is about to enter your path. To avoid a midair collision with the flying reptiles, choose to either divert the reptiles (using Power) or veer away from them.

To divert the reptiles (using Power)*: Use your Force Movement Power. Roll the 20-dice to make the reptiles fly in a direction away from you. Your roll# + your power# + your Power's far-range# is your adventure#.

If your adventure# is equal to or more than 16, add the difference + 10 to your AP total. Changing their course, the reptiles fly away from your vehicle. You may proceed.

If your adventure# is less than 16, subtract the difference from your AP total. You are unable to focus your power on all the flying reptiles. Proceed to veer away from the reptiles (below).

*NOTE: This counts as one of three Power uses you are allowed on this adventure.

To veer away from the reptiles: Roll the 20-dice to steer your vehicle above the flock of flying reptiles. If you are flying a one-person vehicle, your roll# + your navigation# + your vehicle's speed# + your vehicle's stealth# is your adventure#. If you are piloting the shuttle, your roll# + your navigation# + 2 is your adventure#.

If your adventure# is equal to or more than 13, add the difference + 10 to your AP total. Your vehicle rises above the flying reptiles, and you maintain your course for the Cavern of Screaming Skulls. You may proceed.

If your adventure# is less than 13, subtract 5 from your AP total. Just as you are about to fly above the airborne reptiles, the flock ascends! You must push the controls hard to the side. To avoid hitting the flying reptiles, roll the 20-dice again. Your new roll# + your navigation# + your strength# + 2 is your new adventure#.

If your new adventure# is equal to or more than 13, add the difference to your AP total. Pushing the controls hard to the side, you steer the vehicle past the flying reptiles, narrowly missing them. You may proceed.

If your new adventure# is less than 13, subtract the difference from your AP total. The reptiles fly into your path again! Go back "To avoid hitting the flying reptiles," and repeat. When you have maneuvered around the flock, you may proceed.

The mouth of the Cavern of Screaming Skulls is located on a steep slope of Mount Octan. Below the mouth, a rocky shelf protrudes. The shelf appears to be relatively level and a good area on which to land your vehicle. Proceed to land on the rocky shelf.

To land on the rocky shelf: Roll the 10-dice to bring your vehicle down outside the Cavern of Screaming Skulls. If you are flying a one-person vehicle, your roll# + your navigation# + your vehicle's stealth# is your adventure#. If you are piloting the shuttle, your roll# + your navigation# + 1 is your adventure#.

If your adventure# is equal to or more than 9, add the difference + 7 to your AP total. You land your vehicle with expert precision. You may proceed.

If your adventure# is less than 9, subtract 7 from your AP total. A strong wind picks up, blowing your vehicle away from the rocky shelf. It will take a strong grip on the controls to steady your vehicle and land. To make another pass at the landing area, roll the 10-dice again. Your new roll# + your navigation# + your strength# is your new adventure#.

> *If your new adventure# is equal to or more than 9*, add the difference to your AP total. Keeping a strong, steady grip on your vehicle's controls, you make a perfect landing outside the Cavern of Screaming Skulls. You may proceed.

> *If your new adventure# is less than 9*, subtract the difference from your AP total. The wind continues to push at your vehicle. Go back "To make another pass at the landing area," and repeat. When you have landed, you may proceed.

You and your allies have landed on the rocky shelf that rests just below the mouth of the Cavern of Screaming Skulls, a bizarre place that lives up to its name. Millions of years before the arrival of human colonists on Nallastia, the cavern was inhabited by many native mammals and reptiles, some quite large. However, most of these ancient beasts perished during a volcanic eruption that transformed their home into a series of massive lava flow tubes. Now all that remains of them are the fossilized forms of their open jaws and writhing skeletons, embedded in the cavern walls. When wind rushes into the cave, it whistles between the bones and echoes through the tunnels and chambers, producing eerie sounds that resemble the howls of wounded, dying creatures. The sounds alone have stopped even the bravest of warriors from setting foot inside the cavern.

The wind picks up and you hear a horrific wail come from the cavern's mouth. At first, you think the sound is the howling effect of the wind, but then you see a shadowy form spill out of the cavern.

It's a spider. A very, very big one. Each of the creature's eight long legs is as thick as your torso. Without warning, the spider aims its spinnerets and releases a wide spray of sticky filaments at you and your allies.

You must avoid being snared by the large spider. Proceed to leap away from the spider.

To leap away from the spider: Roll the 10-dice to jump. If jumping is one of your talents, your roll# + your stealth# + your strength# + 2 is your adventure#. If jumping is not one of your talents, your roll# + your stealth# + your strength# is your adventure#.

If your adventure# is equal to or more than 10, add the difference + 15 to your AP total. The spider's sprayed filaments fail to catch your leaping form. You may proceed.

If your adventure# is less than 10, subtract 5 from your AP total. You did not leap away in time, and a strand of sprayed filament sticks to one of your boots. To break free from the filament, roll the 10-dice again. Your new roll# + your stealth# + your strength# + 1 is your new adventure#.

If your new adventure# is equal to or more than 10, add the difference to your AP total. With a sharp kick, you free yourself from the sticky filament. You may proceed.

If your new adventure# is less than 10, subtract the difference from your AP total.

The sticky filament is stronger than you thought. You have to try again. Go back "To break free from the filament," and repeat. When you have separated yourself from the sticky filament, you may proceed.

The large spider has snared all but one of your allies in its sprayed filaments. Suddenly, the spider's cephalothorax glows bright green, and it releases an electric charge through the filaments. Your three snared allies are instantly stunned into unconsciousness.

You and one ally remain conscious. Both of you face the spider. It is possible that the spider is a sentient creature that acted defensively when it saw you and your allies. If it is sentient, you might be able to communicate with it. However, it is also possible that the spider is purely a murderous beast who has an appetite for humans.

To stop the spider from causing further damage, choose to either communicate with the spider, combat the spider (using Power), or use a weapon.

To communicate with the spider: Roll the 10-dice to ask the spider to release your allies. If animal handling is one of your talents,

your roll# + your charm# + 2 is your adventure#.
If animal handling is not one of your talents,
your roll# + your charm# is your adventure#.

If your adventure# is equal to or more than 8,
add the difference + 20 to your AP total. The
intelligent spider realizes that you never
meant to harm it, and it apologizes for shock-
ing your allies. The spider informs you that
your allies will be all right, but they'll be
unconscious for at least an hour. After apolo-
gizing again, the spider ambles off up the side
of the mountain. You may proceed.

If your adventure# is less than 8, subtract the
difference from your AP total. The spider
either does not understand your request or
would rather make a meal of you. The spider
singles you out for another attack. Proceed to
either combat the spider with Power (below)
or use a weapon (below).

To combat the spider (using Power)*:
Choose your Force Movement Power. Roll the
10-dice to hurtle a nearby rock and to smack it
into the spider's head. Your roll# + your power#
+ your Power's mid-resist# is your adventure#.

If your adventure# is equal to or more than 9,
add the difference + 20 to your AP total. The

19

rock smashes into the spider's head and knocks out the creature. The spider's limp body tumbles down the mountain. You may proceed.

If your adventure# is less than 9, subtract the difference from your AP total. The spider has a thick exoskeleton, and the rock bounces off the spider's head without causing any damage. Proceed to either use a weapon (below) or, if you haven't already tried, communicate with the spider (above).

*NOTE: This counts as one of three Power uses you are allowed on this adventure.

To use a weapon: Choose your weapon. Roll the 20-dice to aim at one of the spider's legs. Your roll# + your weaponry# + your weapon's mid-range# is your adventure#.

If your adventure# is equal to or more than 15, add the difference + 20 to your AP total. The giant spider screeches as you strike one of its eight legs. Retracting its injured appendage, the creature skitters away from the cavern. You may proceed.

If your adventure# is less than 15, subtract 10 from your AP total. You miss the spider's leg, and the creature prepares to pounce. To move closer and aim at the spider's abdomen, roll the

20-dice again. If defense is one of your talents, your new roll# + your weaponry# + your weapon's close-range# + 2 is your new adventure#. If defense is not one of your talents, your new roll# + your weaponry# + your weapon's close-range# + 1 is your new adventure#.

If your new adventure# is equal to or more than 15, add the difference + 5 to your AP total. Black blood gushes out of the spider's wide abdomen, and the fierce creature tumbles down the mountain. You may proceed.

If your new adventure# is less than 15, subtract the difference from your AP total. You missed again! Go back "To move closer and aim at the spider's abdomen," and repeat. When you have defeated the spider, you may proceed.

You and your conscious ally check on your unconscious allies, who remain entangled in the spider's filaments. You must free their bodies from the sticky filaments and move them into the safety of the V-wing shuttle. Proceed to free your allies.

To free your allies: Roll the 10-dice to pull your allies from the sticky filaments. Your roll# + your strength# + 1 is your adventure#.

If your adventure# is equal to or more than 7, add the difference + 10 to your AP total. You have carefully extracted your allies from the filaments. Proceed to move your allies into the shuttle (below).

If your adventure# is less than 7, subtract the difference from your AP total. Your hands slip on a slick strand of filament. Go back "To free your allies," and repeat.

To move your allies into the shuttle: Roll the 20-dice to carry your stunned allies to the safety of the V-wing's interior without catching the attention of any more spiders. Your roll# + your strength# + 2 is your adventure#.

If your adventure# is equal to or more than 11, add the difference + 5 to your AP total. You deposit your allies within the shuttle. You may proceed.

If your adventure# is less than 11, subtract 5 from your AP total. While carrying one of your allies to the shuttle, you almost stumble over a rock. To move more carefully, roll the 20-dice again. Your new roll# + your stealth# + your strength# is your new adventure#.

If your new adventure# is equal to or more than 13, add the difference to your AP total. All your unconscious allies are safely inside the shuttle. You may proceed.

If your new adventure# is less than 13, subtract the difference from your AP total. While carrying an ally to the transport, you nearly get stuck on a loose strand of the spider's filament. Go back "To move more carefully," and repeat. When your allies are safely inside the V-wing shuttle, you may proceed.

Your unconscious allies may require medical attention. It is quickly decided that your conscious ally will pilot the shuttle back to the fortress, where your injured allies can be treated. You will be left with a one-person vehicle so you can return on your own to the fortress. Before the shuttle departs, you also remove a backpack from the shuttle's cargo bay. When you find the gems, you can carry them in the backpack.

The shuttle departs from the rocky shelf at the mouth of the Cavern of Screaming Skulls. The job of gathering the three power gems is now entirely your responsibility.

Upon entering the mouth of the cave, you see the fossilized remains of many creatures embedded in the cavern walls. A cool wind enters the cave and slips through the gaps in the ancient bones, producing a sound that is indeed chilling, like an inhuman growl mixed with an echoing death cry. Looking at the cavern's walls, you recall the poem that Princess Calvaria recited back at the fortress:

> *Beyond the skulls that scream from walls,*
>
> *The first star rests where giants fell.*
>
> *The second star burns under falls.*
>
> *The third star lives where monsters dwell.*

It is obvious that the first line refers to the cavern's entrance, and you know the three "stars" are actually the power gems. The poem seems to hint at the location of each hidden gem, but because you do not have a map of the Cavern of Screaming Skulls, you would be wise to keep the poem in mind as your quest progresses.

Twenty meters into the cavern, the passage forks off in two directions. Choose to either take the left fork or the right fork.

To take the left fork: Roll the 20-dice. Your roll# + your stealth# + 1 is your adventure#.

If your adventure# is equal to or more than 11, add the difference to your AP total. The left fork brings you through a passage that leads to a high-ceilinged chamber. You arrive there without difficulty. You may proceed.

If your adventure# is less than 11, subtract 5 from your AP total. After taking the left fork, you move through a passage that ends at a wall with a hole in it. It'll be a tight squeeze, but you think you can make it through the hole. To squeeze through the hole, roll the 20-dice again. Your new roll# + your stealth# + 2 is your new adventure#.

> *If your new adventure# is equal to or more than 11*, add the difference to your AP total. Squeezing through the hole, you emerge in a high-ceilinged chamber. You may proceed.

> *If your new adventure# is less than 11*, subtract the difference from your AP total. Unable to squeeze through the hole in the wall, you return to the area where the path forks in two directions. Proceed to take the right fork (below).

To take the right fork: Roll the 20-dice. Your roll# + your stealth# is your adventure#.

If your adventure# is equal to or more than 9, add the difference to your AP total. The right fork brings you through a passage to a high-ceilinged chamber, where you arrive without any trouble. You may proceed.

If your adventure# is less than 9, subtract 10 from your AP total. After taking the right fork, you walk through a passage that leads to a chamber. Unfortunately, a large stone blocks the chamber's entrance, but you think a good, strong push should knock the stone over and allow you to pass. To push the stone, roll the 20-dice again. Your new roll# + your strength# + 2 is your new adventure#.

If your new adventure# is equal to or more than 11, add the difference to your AP total. With a mighty push, you send the stone toppling to the cavern floor, allowing you to enter the inner chamber. You may proceed.

If your new adventure# is less than 11, subtract the difference from your AP total. The stone is heavier than you expected. Go back "To push the stone," and repeat. When the stone has been toppled, you may proceed.

You enter a high-ceilinged, rock-walled chamber that is dominated by an enormous spiderweb. You suspect the web was spun by the same spider that rendered your allies unconscious. As you shine your glow rod around the chamber, you are surprised to hear a high voice rasp, "Help...me!"

You turn to see a short, ratlike creature trapped in the spiderweb. You recognize the creature as a male Ranat, a species with a reputation for savagery and a taste for other intelligent beings. This particular Ranat looks meek and frightened. You ask, "How did you get in here?"

The Ranat's sharp teeth chatter in fear as he replies, "I am a trader from the planet Aralia. When I arrived on Nallastia, the people pretended I was welcome, but then they threw me in this cave! Please free me...before the spider comes back!"

Unless you help the Ranat, the creature might die there. The web appears to be made with the same sticky substance that bound your allies, but when you tug at it, you realize it has solidified into strands that cannot be easily broken.

You set your glow rod on the chamber's floor. To free the Ranat from the web, choose to either use your strength to break the web, or use a weapon.

To use your strength to break the web:
Roll the 10-dice to deliver a sharp chop to the solidified filament that binds the Ranat. Your roll# + your strength# + 3 is your adventure#.

If your adventure# is equal to or more than 9, add the difference + 3 to your AP total. The filament snaps, and the Ranat is freed from the web. You may proceed.

If your adventure# is less than 9, subtract the difference from your AP total. You are not strong enough to break the web with your bare hands. Proceed to use a weapon (below).

To use a weapon: Choose your weapon. Roll the 20-dice to aim at the solidified filament that binds the Ranat. Your roll# + your weaponry# + your weapon's close-range# is your adventure#.

If your adventure# is equal to or more than 15, add the difference + 4 to your AP total. You succeed. You may proceed.

If your adventure# is less than 15, subtract 5 from your AP total. You nearly struck the helpless Ranat. To re-aim at the filament, roll the 20-dice again. Your new roll# + your weaponry# + your weapon's close-range# + 1 is your new adventure#.

If your new adventure# is equal to or more than 15, add the difference to your AP total. Your weapon shatters the solidified filament without harming the Ranat. You may proceed.

If your new adventure# is less than 15, subtract the difference from your AP total. You missed! Go back "To re-aim at the filament," and repeat. When you have freed the Ranat, you may proceed.

"Thanks," says the Ranat. Then the rat-like alien draws a concealed blaster pistol and aims it at you. "Hands up!"

Unsure if the Ranat's mind is in a troubled state, you raise your hands slowly. "I'm not going to hurt you," you say.

The Ranat chuckles. "That's mighty nice of you. See, I lied when I told you the Nallastians threw me in here. They don't even know I'm in their world. I journeyed many light-years to find the legendary power gems, and I'm guessing you want them, too, since there's no other good reason to be in this cave. I don't intend to share the gems, but maybe we can make a deal. If you can spare, say, a few thousand credits, maybe I'll only shoot you with a stunning blast!"

There is no point in continuing this conversation. Choose to either frighten the Ranat (using Power), knock the blaster from the Ranat's grip, or use a weapon.

To frighten the Ranat (using Power)*: Choose your Persuasion or Alteration Power. Roll the 20-dice to make the Ranat think the giant spider has returned to the chamber. Your roll# + your power# + your Power's mid-resist# is your adventure#.

If your adventure# is equal to or more than 12, add the difference + 15 to your AP total. Screaming for mercy, the Ranat fears he won't be safe from the spider until he leaves the cavern, returns to his spaceship, and flees Nallastia, never to return. The Ranat dashes out of the cavern. You may proceed.

If your adventure# is less than 12, subtract the difference from your AP total. The idiotic Ranat is immune to fear. Proceed to knock the blaster from the Ranat's grip (below), or use a weapon (below).

*NOTE: This counts as one of three Power uses you are allowed on this adventure.

To knock the blaster from the Ranat's grip: Roll the 10-dice to kick the Ranat's hand.

If martial arts is one of your talents, your roll# + your strength# + 3 is your adventure#. If martial arts is not one of your talents, your roll# + your strength# + 1 is your adventure#.

If your adventure# is equal to or more than 8, add the difference + 15 to your AP total. Your foot connects with the Ranat's wrist, and he drops his blaster. The defenseless Ranat flees from the cavern and leaves in his spaceship. You may proceed.

If your adventure# is less than 8, subtract the difference from your AP total. The Ranat dodges your kick and prepares to fire his blaster at you. Proceed to use a weapon (below) or to frighten the Ranat using Power (above).

To use a weapon: Choose your weapon. Roll the 20-dice to aim at the Ranat's blaster arm. Your roll# + your weaponry# + your weapon's mid-range# is your adventure#.

If your adventure# is equal to or more than 14, add the difference to your AP total. You have disabled the Ranat's blaster arm, and he drops his weapon. Fearing for his life, the ill-mannered Ranat flees from the cavern, returns to his spaceship, and leaves Nallastia as fast as he can. You may proceed.

If your adventure# is less than 14, subtract 5 from your AP total. You missed the Ranat's blaster arm—and he squeezes off a shot! To dodge the fired laser bolt, roll the 20-dice again. Your new roll# + your stealth# + 2 is your new adventure#.

If your new adventure# is equal to or more than 13, add the difference to your AP total. The fired laser bolt whizzes past your head and hits the chamber's wall. Go back "To use a weapon," and repeat. When you have defeated the Ranat, you may proceed.

If your new adventure# is less than 13, subtract the difference from your AP total. The laser bolt nicked you—and the Ranat fires again! Go back "To dodge the fired laser bolt," and repeat. When you have dodged the laser bolt and defeated the Ranat, you may proceed.

Picking up your glow rod, you leave the web-filled chamber and proceed through a low-ceilinged tunnel. You aim your glow rod at the tunnel's floor, watching for any stones or slick spots that might cause you to trip or slip. After walking about thirty meters, you see that the tunnel appears to end in total darkness.

Moving cautiously toward the darkness, you realize the tunnel empties abruptly over a deep chasm. Your glow rod is capable of illuminating objects up to fifty meters away, and you can see a wide wall on the other side of the chasm, about fifteen meters from you. You extend the rod out over the floor's edge, but the chasm's walls vanish into a distant black area. You can only imagine the chasm's depth.

To your lower right, you see what appears to be a natural bridge that extends over the chasm to another dark hole, possibly a tunnel. You are considering whether you might be able to jump to the bridge when you notice a long, narrow ledge just below your position. The ledge travels down along the wall to the bridge.

You clip the glow rod to your belt. To reach the bridge, choose to either scale the ledge or jump to the bridge.

To scale the ledge: Roll the 10-dice to climb down to the bridge. Your roll# + your stealth# + your strength# is your adventure#.

If your adventure# is equal to or more than 9, add the difference + 8 to your AP total. Moving cautiously along the ledge, you reach the bridge that spans the underground chasm. You may proceed.

If your adventure# is less than 9, subtract 5 from your AP total. You nearly slip off the ledge, but quickly regain your balance. To continue on the ledge, roll the 10-dice again. Your new roll# + your stealth# + your strength# + 1 is your new adventure#.

> *If your new adventure# is equal to or more than 9*, add the difference to your AP total. Easing yourself off the ledge, you step onto the bridge. You may proceed.

> *If your new adventure# is less than 9*, subtract the difference from your AP total. You almost slipped again! Proceed to jump to the bridge (below).

To jump to the bridge: Roll the 20-dice to leap down to the bridge that spans the subterranean chasm. If jumping is one of your talents, your roll# + your strength# + 3 is your adventure#. If jumping is not one of your talents, your roll# + your strength# + 1 is your adventure#.

If your adventure# is equal to or more than 13, add the difference + 3 to your AP total. Leaping through the darkness, you land on the bridge. You may proceed.

If your adventure# is less than 13, subtract 5 from your AP total. You land on the bridge, but lose your balance and start to fall off! To regain your balance, roll the 20-dice again. Your new roll# + your stealth# + your strength# is your new adventure#.

If your new adventure# is equal to or more than 15, add the difference to your AP total. Regaining your balance, you breathe a sigh of relief. You may proceed.

If your new adventure# is less than 15, subtract the difference from your AP total. You still have not regained your balance. Go back "To regain your balance," and repeat. When your feet are firmly planted on the bridge, you may proceed.

The bridge has many cracks running through it, but it looks stable enough. You begin to walk across it, moving toward the other side of the chasm where you can see the entrance to the next tunnel. You are halfway across the bridge when you hear a *click* as a layer of stone yields to your weight and shifts below your feet. Then you hear another *click* behind you, and you turn your head to face the chasm wall at your back, where a small area of the wall slides to the side and reveals a round hole.

The hole contains an ancient wall-mounted laser projector. Evidently, your weight on the bridge has triggered an old automated laser trap. The projector's targeting sensor glows red.

Trapped halfway across the bridge, you are dead in the laser projector's sights. You know you cannot reach the next tunnel before the laser projector fires. You also know that jumping off the bridge would almost certainly prove fatal.

The laser projector fires. Choose to either duck, leap high above the bridge, or deflect the laser bolt.

To duck: Roll the 10-dice to quickly lower yourself close to the bridge's surface. Your roll# + your stealth# is your adventure#.

If your adventure# is equal to or more than 6, add the difference + 10 to your AP total. The laser bolt sails over your head and hits the other side of the chasm. Fortunately, the single shot has drained the old laser projector's energy. You stand up. You may proceed.

If your adventure# is less than 6, subtract the difference from your AP total. The first laser bolt misses, but the laser projector has fired another shot directly at you. Proceed to leap high above the bridge (below) or deflect the laser bolt (below).

To leap high above the bridge: Roll the 10-dice to jump. If jumping is one of your talents, your roll# + your strength# + 2 is your adventure#. If jumping is not one of your talents, your roll# + your strength# is your adventure#.

If your adventure# is equal to or more than 8, add the difference to your AP total. After you jump, the laser bolt sails under your feet and impacts against the wall on the other side of the chasm. Fortunately, the single shot has drained the old laser projector's energy. You land on the bridge. You may proceed.

If your adventure# is less than 8, subtract the difference from your AP total. You jump and the laser bolt misses your body, but when you touch back down on the bridge, the laser projector draws a bead on you and fires again. Proceed to deflect the laser bolt (below).

To deflect the laser bolt: Choose your weapon. Roll the 20-dice to strike the oncoming bolt. If defense is one of your talents, your roll# + your weaponry# + your weapon's mid-range#

+ 1 is your adventure#. If defense is not one of your talents, your roll# + your weaponry# + your weapon's mid-range# is your adventure#.

If your adventure# is equal to or more than 15, add the difference + 10 to your AP total. Using your weapon, you slam the fired bolt straight back at the laser projector. The projector is destroyed, and you may proceed.

If your adventure# is less than 15, subtract 6 from your AP total. Using your weapon, you manage to deflect the fired bolt, but the laser projector prepares to fire another bolt straight at you. To aim at the laser projector, roll the 20-dice again. Your new roll# + your weaponry# + your weapon's far-range# is your new adventure#.

If your new adventure# is equal to or more than 14, add the difference + 5 to your AP total. You successfully deflect the fired bolt straight back at the laser projector. It is destroyed. You may proceed.

If your new adventure# is less than 14, subtract the difference from your AP total. You deflect the fired bolt, but yet another is coming right at you. Go back "To aim at the laser projector," and repeat. When you have destroyed the laser projector, you may proceed.

After crossing the bridge to the other side of the chasm, you enter a tunnel that delivers you to another high-ceilinged chamber. To your amazement, the chamber's walls are lined with enormous statues of alien beings, some standing over eight meters high. If the statues are faithful likenesses, the beasts were insect-like creatures with four arms and two multi-faceted eyes.

There are fourteen statues in all, twelve of which are upright; the remaining two lie across the floor, broken into many pieces. At first, you suspect the shattered pair might have been deliberately toppled, but then you notice a wide, heaving crack in the chamber's floor, right under the area where the two fallen statues once stood. It appears an earthquake might be to blame for bringing down the statues.

The statues are much older than any artifacts on Nallastia's surface, indicating that an alien civilization existed on the moon long before the arrival of human colonists. You cannot help but wonder if the creatures died off or emigrated elsewhere, but you push aside these thoughts to concentrate on your mission. You are making your way past the statues, heading for a doorway that looks like a passage to another chamber, when you remember...

The first star rests where giants fell.

You look back at the two fallen statues. Could these be the "giants" of the poem? You walk to the statues that lie on the floor and search for any sign of the first power gem. Trying to imagine where Nallastia Octan might have hidden the gem, you look at the wide crack in the floor and notice that it opens up into a gaping hole. Extending your glow rod, you peer down into the hole. Instead of seeing a gem, you find yourself gazing into the golden eyes of a large serpent!

Stepping backward, you stumble on a stone. The serpent springs up through the hole with its wide jaws open, baring long fangs. The serpent rears its head, flicks its tongue, and prepares to swallow you whole.

You must defeat the serpent. Choose to either throw a stone into the serpent's mouth, punch the serpent's snout, or use a weapon.

To throw a stone into the serpent's mouth: Roll the 20-dice to pick up a stone and hurl it at the large serpent. Your roll# + your strength# + 1 is your adventure#.

If your adventure# is equal to or more than 13, add the difference + 20 to your AP total. The stone slams into the serpent's mouth, causing it to choke and shattering one of its fangs. The serpent slithers away from you and hides in a distant corner. You may proceed.

If your adventure# is less than 13, subtract the difference from your AP total. The serpent sways hard to the side and the stone breezes past the creature. The serpent hisses, then strikes out at you. Proceed to punch the serpent's snout (below) or use a weapon (below).

To punch the serpent's snout: Roll the 10-dice to throw a devastating punch at the serpent. If defense or martial arts is one of your talents, your roll# + your strength# + your skill# is your adventure#. If defense or martial arts is not one of your talents, your roll# + your strength# is your adventure#.

If your adventure# is equal to or more than 9, add the difference + 20 to your AP total. Wham! You hit the serpent square on its snout. The serpent weaves, then its body crashes to the floor. The creature is out like a light, and you may proceed.

If your adventure# is less than 9, subtract 5 from your AP total. Your punch glances off the serpent's jaw...which only angers the large reptile. To throw another punch, roll the 10-dice again. Your new roll# + your strength# + + 1 is your new adventure#.

If your new adventure# is equal to or more than 9, add the difference to your AP total. You throw all your weight into the punch, which produces a nasty sounding *crunch* when it connects with the serpent's snout. Sounded like a bone breaking. Fortunately, the bone was not one of yours. The snake collapses to the chamber floor, and you may proceed.

If your new adventure# is less than 9, subtract the difference from your AP total. The serpent dodges your punch, then prepares to knock you down with its tail. Proceed to use a weapon (below).

To use a weapon: Choose your weapon. Roll the 20-dice to aim at the large serpent. Your roll# + your weaponry# + your weapon's mid-range# is your adventure#.

If your adventure# is equal to or more than 14, add the difference + 20 to your AP total.

The serpent is no match for your expert use of weaponry. You may proceed.

If your adventure# is less than 14, subtract 5 from your AP total. You miss, and now the serpent is almost on top of you! To move closer and make another strike at the serpent, roll the 20-dice again. Your new roll# + your stealth# + your weaponry# + your weapon's close-range# is your new adventure#.

> *If your new adventure# is equal to or more than 16*, add the difference to your AP total. You strike down the serpent, and it flops to the floor with a loud *thud*. You may proceed.

> *If your new adventure# is less than 16*, subtract the difference from your AP total. You miss again! Go back "To move closer and make another strike at the serpent," and repeat. When you defeat the serpent, you may proceed.

Hoping you won't encounter any more serpents, you risk another look into the hole in the chamber's cracked floor. This time, you see a beautiful blue gem in the area that was occupied by the serpent. An old, dust-covered spear also rests in the hole. Both the gem and the spear are within arm's reach. You try to pick up the gem, but discover it is stuck, partially wedged between two layers of rock.

To remove the gem from the rocks, choose to either pull the gem free, use the old spear as a lever, or use a weapon to pulverize the upper layer of rock.

To pull the gem free: Roll the 10-dice to reach into the hole and lift the power gem. Your roll# + your strength# is your adventure#.

If your adventure# is equal to or more than 8, add the difference to your AP total. Without any difficulty, you remove the blue power gem from the hole. You may proceed.

If your adventure# is less than 8, subtract 5 from your AP total. The gem does not budge. To use more technique, roll the 10-dice again. Your new roll# + your strength# + your skill# is your new adventure#.

If your new adventure# is equal to or more than 8, add the difference to your AP total. Free from its hiding place, the power gem is now in your hands. You may proceed.

If your new adventure# is less than 8, subtract the difference from your AP total.

You can't get a good grip on the power gem. Proceed to either use the old spear as a lever (below) or use a weapon to pulverize the upper layer of rock (below).

To use the old spear as a lever: Roll the 20-dice to drive the spear under the rock that pins the power gem, then lift. Your roll# + your skill# + your strength# is your adventure#.

If your adventure# is equal to or more than 13, add the difference to your AP total. Pressing down on the spear, you manage to work the power gem out from under the rock. You pick up the gem, and you may proceed.

If your adventure# is less than 13, subtract the difference from your AP total. The old spear snaps in half. Proceed to use a weapon to pulverize the upper layer of rock (below), or pull the gem free, if you haven't already tried that (above).

To use a weapon to pulverize the upper layer of rock: Choose your weapon. Roll the 20-dice to break the rock into small pieces. Your roll# + your weaponry# + your weapon's close-range# is your adventure#.

If your adventure# is equal to or more than 14, add the difference to your AP total.

Shattering the rock into tiny bits, you are able to extract the power gem from the rubble. You may proceed.

If your adventure# is less than 14, subtract 6 from your AP total. The rock is harder than you thought. To take another crack at the rock, roll the 20-dice again. Your new roll# + your weaponry# + your weapon's close-range# + 1 is your new adventure#.

If your new adventure# is equal to or more than 14, add the difference to your AP total. The upper layer of rock is reduced to small bits of rubble, allowing you to pick up the power gem. You may proceed.

If your new adventure# is less than 14, subtract the difference from your AP total. You still can't shatter the rock. Try again. Go back "To take another crack at the rock," and repeat. When you have shattered the rock that holds down the power gem, you may proceed.

The blue power gem seems to glow as you hold it in your hand. Placing the gem in your backpack, you leave the statue-filled chamber and move on to the next passage.

You have the first power gem. Add 50 to your AP total.

The passage is lined with smooth walls made of a strong, highly reflective alloy. The ceiling appears to be made of the same material. With their reflective quality, the ceiling and walls intensify the light of your glow rod so much that the brightness impairs your vision. Proceed to dim your glow rod.

To dim your glow rod: Roll the 10-dice to adjust a twist dial on your glow rod's handle. Your roll# + your skill# is your adventure#.

If your adventure# is equal to or more than 5, add the difference to your AP total. Twisting the intensity control on your glow rod's handle, you dim the light so it is easier on your eyes. You may proceed.

If your adventure# is less than 5, subtract the difference from your AP total. Twisting the intensity control on your glow rod's handle, you accidentally increase the brightness. Despite this setback, you now know how to adjust the device. To twist the dial in the other direction, roll the 10-dice again. Your new roll# + your knowledge# + your skill# is your new adventure#.

If your new adventure# is equal to or more than 6, add the difference to your AP total. The light dims to a level that does not cause any discomfort to your eyes. You may proceed.

If your new adventure# is less than 6, subtract the difference from your AP total. You lose your grip on your glow rod. Go back "To twist the dial in the other direction," and repeat. When you have reduced the brightness emitted by your glow rod, you may proceed.

With your glow rod adjusted to a dimmer setting, you move forward through the passage, leaving a trail of footprints on the dusty floor. Soon, you are startled to see a shadowy humanoid figure—also carrying a glow rod—approaching from the other direction. You quickly realize that this approaching figure is only your own reflection on a metal wall where the passage makes a sharp right-angle turn.

Following the turn, you soon arrive at another turn, and then another and another. The combination of the walls' reflective surfaces and the numerous turns serve to confuse your sense of direction, leaving you uncertain of which way you are heading. After several more turns, the passage ends at a metal door that is made of the same alloy as the walls.

A slender lever appears to be the door's opening mechanism. You press down on the lever and hear a *clack* but the door does not open. Perhaps you handled the lever the wrong way and accidentally locked the door, or maybe the opening mechanism is jammed.

The door appears to be made of the same reflective alloy as the walls and ceiling. You do not know what effect an energy weapon might have on the alloy, but you suspect a blaster bolt would ricochet. To open the metal door, choose to either pull the lever up, hot-wire the lock, or kick the door in.

To pull the lever up: Roll the 10-dice to lift the lever. Your roll# + your strength# is your adventure#.

If your adventure# is equal to or more than 6, add the difference + 10 to your AP total. You lift the lever and the door opens without difficulty. You may proceed.

If your adventure# is less than 6, subtract the difference from your AP total. Over many centuries, the lever has become incredibly brittle, and it breaks off in your hands. Proceed to either hot-wire the lock (below) or kick the door in (below).

To hot-wire the lock: Roll the 20-dice to manipulate the locking mechanism. If repair is one of your talents, your roll# + your knowledge# + your skill# + 2 is your adventure#. If repair is not one of your talents, your roll# + your knowledge# + your skill# is your adventure#.

If your adventure# is equal to or more than 15, add the difference + 5 to your AP total. The tumblers release the bolts that secure the lock, and the door opens. You may proceed.

If your adventure# is less than 15, subtract 5 from your AP total. This lock is proving difficult, but you still think you can open it. To give it another try, roll the 20-dice again. Your new roll# + your knowledge# + your skill# + 1 is your new adventure#.

If your new adventure# is equal to or more than 15, add the difference to your AP total. You have hot-wired the lock, and the door opens. You may proceed.

If your new adventure# is less than 15, subtract the difference from your AP total.

The lock cannot be picked, at least not by human fingers. Proceed to kick the door in (below).

To kick the door in: Roll the 20-dice to place a powerful kick at the door's center. If martial arts is one of your talents, your roll# + your strength# + 2 is your adventure#. If martial arts is not one of your talents, your roll# + your strength# + 1 is your adventure#.

If your adventure# is equal to or more than 12, add the difference + 5 to your AP total. With a single kick, you open the door. You may proceed.

If your adventure# is less than 12, subtract 5 from your AP total. You didn't even dent the door. To launch a more powerful kick, roll the 20-dice again. Your new roll# + your strength# + 2 is your new adventure#.

If your new adventure# is equal to or more than 12, add the difference to your AP total. Yielding to the force of your kick, the door opens. You may proceed.

If your new adventure# is less than 12, subtract the difference from your AP total. It still won't open. You need to kick even harder. Go back "To launch a more power-ful kick," and repeat. When you have kicked the door open, you may proceed.

Passing through the open doorway, you enter a ten-sided chamber with a dust-free grated floor and ten mirrored walls. On each wall, there is a closed door, except for the open doorway behind you, which leads back the way you came. But as you step to the center of the chamber, you hear a *slam* and turn to see that the door behind you has closed automatically.

All of the doors are identical, without any marks to distinguish one from another, and all are made of the same reflective alloy as the walls. The only source of light is from your glow rod. All the reflections are disori-enting. Hoping to regain your bearings, you consider marking the door through which you entered, but then you realize you can no longer identify even *that* one. The grated dust-free floor prevents you from retracing your footsteps.

You look down at the grates, then peer through the small, open gaps between the lattices. It looks like there is a stone-walled chamber about three meters below your position, but you cannot see if it leads to another passage.

You do not know whether you have entered a trap set by Nallastia Octan or an ancient alien fun house. Maybe you're wrong on both counts. All you know for certain is that the Trinity Stones are still closing in on the Firewells back at the fortress. You have to keep moving.

There are ten doors in the chamber. Proceed to open a door.

To open a door: Roll the 10-dice. Your roll# is your adventure#.

If you roll 1, subtract 5 from your AP total. You have opened the door that leads back the way you came. Go back "To open a door," and repeat.

If you roll 2, add 5 to your AP total. The door opens into a mirrored passage that twists and turns several times before you arrive at another door. To open this door, roll the 20-dice for your new adventure#.

If your new adventure# is equal to or more than 11, add the difference + 5 to your AP total. The door opens to a passage that does not have mirrored walls. You may proceed.

If your new adventure# *is less than 11*, subtract 6 from your AP total. Opening the door, you learn that the twisting passage has led you back into the ten-sided chamber. You're simultaneously angry and impressed with the ancient architect who designed this maze of mirrors. Go back "To open a door," and repeat.

If you roll 3, subtract 10 from your AP total. Disoriented, you accidentally tried to open a reflection of a door! Go back "To open a door," and repeat.

If you roll 4, add 25 to your AP total. You are greatly relieved when you open the door and step into a passage that does not have mirrored walls. You may proceed.

If you roll 5, subtract 13 from your AP total. The door opens to a stone wall. Go back "To open a door," and repeat.

If you roll 6, add 5 to your AP total. The door opens to a spiral staircase that descends into darkness. Leaving the chamber with the grated floor, you wind your way down the stairs. At the bottom of the stairs, you find another door. To open this door, roll the 20-dice for your new adventure#.

If your new adventure# is equal to or more than 11, add the difference + 10 to your AP total. Opening the door at the bottom of the stairs, you step into a passage that does not have mirrored walls. You may proceed.

If your new adventure# is less than 11, subtract 5 from your AP total. The door opens to a stone-walled chamber. When you look up, you see the ceiling is actually the grated floor of the ten-sided chamber that you just left. The lower level does not lead anywhere, so you ascend the spiral staircase and return to the chamber. Go back "To open a door," and repeat.

If you roll 7, subtract 7 from your AP total. Disoriented, you thought you were stepping toward a door when you accidentally bumped into one of the mirrored walls. Go back "To open a door," and repeat.

If you roll 8, do not add or subtract any points to your AP total. You are so disoriented, you have to close your eyes and give your mind a short rest. Seconds later, your head is clear. Go back "To open a door," and repeat.

If you roll 9, add 10 to your AP total. The door opens into an old cylindrical lift tube.

Stepping into the lift tube, you see it travels between two levels, and that you are currently on the lower one. To push a switch that will send the lift to the upper level, roll the 20-dice for your new adventure#.

If your new adventure# is equal to or more than 11, add the difference + 5 to your AP total. Seconds after you push the switch, you arrive at the upper level. There you are greatly relieved when the lift tube's door opens to a passage that does not have mirrored walls. You may proceed.

If your new adventure# is less than 11, subtract 15 from your AP total. You push the switch and it snaps off. This old lift hasn't gone up or down for thousands of years, and you doubt it will be traveling in any direction in the near future. Go back "To open a door," and repeat.

If you roll 0, add 25 to your AP total. You are greatly relieved when you open the door and step into a passage that does not have mirrored walls. You may proceed.

As you leave the dizzying chamber of mirrors and doors, you feel some relief to be walking through a passage with nonreflective stone walls. The passage leads to the largest chamber yet, a cavern with well-preserved natural features. The only evidence of an ancient alien presence is a time worn path that weaves around the many stalagmites that rise from the floor. Long stalactites dangle from the high ceiling, and you imagine that you might have a similar view from inside the jaws of a gigantic carnivorous animal.

Your glow rod casts bizarre shadows as you walk quietly along the path. The sound of dripping water reaches your ears, but, because of the numerous natural formations of stone that surround you, the sound seems to echo in all directions and you are unable to pinpoint its origin. When the path rounds a towering stalagmite, you emerge at the edge of a subterranean lake. There you see the source of the sound: Water is dripping from the smooth edge of a wide, sloping stone that extends from a wall and juts out over the lake.

Each drip sends a gentle ripple across the lake's surface. By the light of your glow rod, the water is so clear that you can easily see multi-colored rocks that rest at the bottom of the basin. Looking at the smooth edge of the wide stone from which the water drips, you suspect the stone may have been contoured by a waterfall over the course of many centuries.

Suddenly, the words come to you: *The second star burns under falls.*

Keeping your eyes on the area of the lake below the smooth-edged stone, you move your glow rod behind a nearby stalactite so the lake is once again in darkness. Under the water's surface, at the bottom of the basin, a glowing red gem becomes visible among the multi-colored rocks. You could not see it before because its color and luminescence were diminished by the light of your glow rod.

You must obtain the second power gem. Choose to either make the gem rise out of the lake (using Power) or dive for the gem.

To make the gem rise out of the lake (using Power)*: Choose your Force Movement Power. Roll the 20-dice to bring the gem up from the bottom of the subterranean lake. Your roll# + your power# + your Power's mid-resist# is your adventure#.

If your adventure# is equal to or more than 12, add the difference + 10 to your AP total. The red power gem travels up through the lake's cold water until it breaks the surface, then it flies to your waiting hand. You may proceed.

If your adventure# is less than 12, subtract 10 from your AP total. Perhaps your mind is still muddied by your recent experience in the chamber of mirrors, but you are having some trouble getting a mental lock on the submerged power gem. You might do better if you close your eyes. To concentrate on the power gem with your eyes closed, roll the 20-dice again. Your new roll# + your power# + your Power's high-resist# is your new adventure#.

> *If your new adventure# is equal to or more than 13*, add the difference to your AP total. The power gem rises out of the water, travels through the air, and lands in your waiting hand. You may proceed.

> *If your new adventure# is less than 13*, subtract the difference from your AP total. Even with your eyes closed, you are unable to focus your power on the submerged power gem. Proceed to dive for the gem (below).

*NOTE: This counts as one of three Power uses you are allowed on this adventure.

To dive for the gem: Roll the 20-dice to plunge to the bottom of the subterranean lake. Your roll# + your strength# + your stealth# is your adventure#.

If your adventure# is equal to or more than 14, add the difference + 10 to your AP total. At the bottom of the lake, you remove the power gem from the neighboring multi-colored rocks, then carry the gem back to the shore. You may proceed.

If your adventure# is less than 14, subtract 5 from your AP total. You swim down to the bottom of the lake, reach for the power gem, and accidentally grab one of the multi-colored rocks. You don't realize your mistake until you reach the water's surface. The power gem remains at the bottom of the lake. To make another dive, roll the 20-dice again. Your new roll# + your strength# + your stealth# + 1 is your new adventure#.

If your new adventure# is equal to or more than 14, add the difference to your AP total. This time, you grab the power gem and return with it to the lake's shore. You may proceed.

If your new adventure# is less than 14, subtract the difference from your AP total.

Again, you grabbed the wrong stone. Go back "To make another dive," and repeat. When you have retrieved the red power gem from the bottom of the lake, you may proceed.

Facing away from the lake, you stand at the water's edge and smile as you hold the second power gem.

For retrieving the second power gem, reward yourself with 40 AP.

You clip your glow rod to your belt and are about to place the gem in your backpack when something strikes against the back of your legs, knocking you down into the water. A rough appendage coils around your wrist and you feel the gem being torn from your grip.

At first, you think you have been attacked by another serpent, but when you turn to face your attacker, you realize that you are in the clutches of a multi-tentacled aquatic creature that now also holds the red power gem. Keeping its grip on your wrist, the creature quickly slaps a tentacle around your neck and tosses the red gem into its beak-like mouth, which is encircled by six large, purple eyes. Before you can protest, the creature tightens its hold on your neck. Your first encounter with this life-form is not going at all well.

The tentacled creature might be intelligent, in which case you could communicate with it. Another option is to temporarily blind the creature by shining your glow rod directly into its large, light-sensitive eyes. Then again, the creature might only release you if you give it a solid punch or use a weapon.

You must make the creature release you and relinquish the red power gem. Choose to either communicate with the creature, shine your glow rod in the creature's eyes, punch the creature's beak, or use a weapon.

To communicate with the creature: Roll the 20-dice. If animal handling is one of your talents, your roll# + your charm# + your knowledge# is your adventure#. If animal handling is not one of your talents, your roll# + your charm# is your adventure#.

If your adventure# is equal to or more than 13, add the difference + 18 to your AP total. The creature realizes you are friendly and that you have a good reason to want the power gem. Coughing up the gem, the creature returns it to you and wishes you good luck. You may proceed.

If your adventure# is less than 13, subtract the difference from your AP total. Oblivious to your attempt at communication, the creature tightens its grip on your neck. Proceed to either shine your glow rod in the creature's eyes (below), punch the creature's beak (below), or use a weapon (below).

To shine your glow rod in the creature's eyes: Use your glow rod as a weapon. Roll the 10-dice to temporarily blind the creature. Your roll# + your stealth# + 1 is your adventure#.

If your adventure# is equal to or more than 8, add the difference + 17 to your AP total. The aquatic creature's six pupils dilate to painful proportions, causing the beast to shriek and spit up the swallowed power gem before it releases you from its clutches. The temporarily blinded creature slinks off into the dark lake. You may proceed.

If your adventure# is less than 8, subtract the difference from your AP total. The creature must have sensed what you were about to do, because it shuts its eyes before you can use the glow rod to temporarily blind it. Proceed to either communicate with the creature (above) if you have not already tried, punch the creature's beak (below), or use a weapon (below).

To punch the creature's beak: Roll the 10-dice to throw a punch. Your roll# + your strength# + 1 is your adventure#.

If your adventure# is equal to or more than 8, add the difference to your AP total. Your punch connects and the creature's beak reflexively opens, giving you the chance to reach into its mouth and yank out the power gem. Fearing another punch, the creature releases you and swims away. You may proceed.

If your adventure# is less than 8, subtract 5 from your AP total. The creature shifts its head before you can punch its beak. To throw another punch, roll the 10-dice again. Your new roll# + your strength# + 1 is your new adventure#.

If your new adventure# is equal to or more than 10, add the difference to your AP total. You punch the creature's beak and it coughs up the power gem. Afraid you will hit it again, the creature releases its tentacles from your body and swims off into the lake's darkest depths. You may proceed.

If your new adventure# is less than 10, subtract the difference from your AP total. The aquatic creature is completely unfazed by your punch. Proceed to use a weapon (below).

To use a weapon: Choose your weapon. Roll the 20-dice to aim for the creature's tentacles. Your roll# + your weaponry# + your weapon's close-range# is your adventure#.

If your adventure# is equal to or more than 14, add the difference to your AP total. Using your weapon, you relieve the aquatic creature of two tentacles. The creature shrieks as it releases you, and you reach into its open mouth and yank out the red power gem. The wounded creature swims away as fast as it can. You may proceed.

If your adventure# is less than 14, subtract 5 from your AP total. Despite your close proximity to the aquatic creature's body, you are unable to hit even one of its tentacles. The creature squeezes your neck even tighter, and you feel as if you are about to black out. Your only chance of survival is to end the creature's life. To slay the aquatic creature, roll the 20-dice again. Your new roll# + your weaponry# + your weapon's close-range# +1 is your new adventure#.

If your new adventure# is equal to or more than 15, add the difference to your AP total. The creature is dead. As its beak goes slack, out tumbles the red power gem. You may proceed.

If your new adventure# is less than 15, subtract the difference from your AP total. You missed. Go back "To slay the aquatic creature," and repeat. When you have vanquished the murderous beast, you may proceed.

You have the second power gem. Add 50 to your AP total.

After placing the second power gem in your backpack, you leave the subterranean lake. Returning to the walkway that weaves between the many stalactites, you continue your journey through the cavern.

Just off the walkway, there is a dark shadow against a rocky wall that appears to be the entrance to another passage. But as you draw closer to the shadowed spot, you see that it is not an entrance at all, but merely an empty gap between two large boulders that rest against the cavern's wall.

Returning to the walkway, you see that the passage to the next chamber is straight ahead. You are about to step toward the next passage when you feel the ground begin to shake. The cavern is being hit by a seismic tremor. Overhead, there is a cracking sound, and you see several massive, sharp-tipped stalactites break away from the ceiling.

You do not want to be hit by a falling stalactite, nor do you want to become trapped within the cavern. Choose to either dive for cover or run to the next passage.

To dive for cover: Roll the 10-dice to leap into the empty gap between the two large boulders that rest against the cavern's wall. Your roll# + your stealth# is your adventure#.

If your adventure# is equal to or more than 12, add the difference to your AP total. You leap into the gap between the boulders. Seconds later, the tremor ends, allowing you safe access to the next passage. You may proceed.

If your adventure# is less than 12, subtract 5 from your AP total. Before you can dive for cover, a wide stalactite falls from the ceiling and crashes down in front of you, blocking your path to the gap between the two large stones. Proceed to run to the next passage (below).

To run to the next passage: Roll the 20-dice to race for the passage at the end of the path. Your roll# + your stealth# + your strength# is your adventure#.

If your adventure# is equal to or more than 15, add the difference to your AP total. Dodging several falling stalactites, you reach the safety of the next passage just as the tremor ends. You may proceed.

If your adventure# is less than 15, subtract 6 from your AP total. A large stalactite crashes down on the path in front of you, and the tremor continues. The only way you can reach the safety of the next passage is by leaping over the debris that lies on the path. To leap over the debris, roll the 20-dice again. If jumping is one of your talents, your new roll# + your stealth# + your strength# + 1 is your new adventure#. If jumping is not one of your talents, your new roll# + your stealth# + your strength# is your new adventure#.

If your new adventure# is equal to or more than 16, add the difference to your AP total. Leaping over the debris, you enter the next passage just as the tremor ends. You may proceed.

If your new adventure# is less than 16, subtract the difference from your AP total. You didn't leap far enough. Go back "To leap over the debris," and repeat. When you have reached the safety of the next passage, you may proceed.

As you walk through the passage, you see that its walls feature engraved hieroglyphics—pictures and symbols that illustrate the history of the ancient insectoid civilization that constructed the underground chambers. One sequence of hieroglyphs shows the insectoids welcoming a starship that brings humanoid aliens, followed by the insectoids inviting the aliens to a grand banquet; at the banquet, the insectoids reveal their true nature when they round up their guests and prepare them as the main course. In sickening detail, the hieroglyphs show the monstrous insectoids devouring all the aliens.

Looking at the hieroglyphs, you contemplate the poem that hints at the location of each power gem. *The third star lives where monsters dwell.* You wonder if "the monsters" could be living creatures that might have survived through the ages, or if the "monsters" might be symbolic, like the "giants" of *The first star rests where giants fell.*

Hoping you won't encounter any real, living monsters, you continue walking through the passage until you enter another spacious subterranean chamber with stalactites dangling from the ceiling. At the chamber's center, a transparisteel case encloses a pedestal, on which rests a green power gem. The enclosed pedestal is ringed by three stone statues of tall insectoid aliens. If these statues are the monsters mentioned in the poem, it seems you won't have to worry about them.

Loose stones line a walkway that curves around the transparisteel case and leads to another dark passage. Stepping past the stones, you move closer to the transparisteel case. As its name implies, transparisteel is transparent metal, a material typically used for viewports on starships. Although transparisteel is generally quite strong, this particular case looks old and quite brittle. On the side of the case, there is a dial that appears to be the case's opening mechanism.

To obtain the green power gem, you must open the transparisteel case. Choose to either twist the case's dial, throw a stone at the case, or use a weapon.

To twist the case's dial: Roll the 20-dice to twist the dial. Your roll# + your skill# is your adventure#.

If your adventure# is equal to or more than 13, add the difference + 10 to your AP total. When the dial on the side of the case is twisted, the transparisteel panels slide down into the floor, leaving the pedestal and green power gem exposed. You remove the power gem from the case, and you may proceed.

If your adventure# is less than 13, subtract 10 from your AP total. You twisted the dial in the wrong direction, but you now know the correct way to turn it. To twist the dial in the opposite direction, roll the 20-dice again. Your new roll# + your knowledge# + your skill# is your new adventure#.

If your new adventure# is equal to or more than 14, add the difference to your AP total. After you twist the dial in the opposite direction, the case's transparisteel panels slide back, allowing you to pick up the green power gem. You may proceed.

If your new adventure# is less than 14, subtract the difference from your AP total. The dial won't turn in the opposite direction, and the transparisteel case remains sealed. Proceed to either throw a stone at the case (below) or use a weapon (below).

To throw a stone at the case: Roll the 10-dice to pick up one of the loose stones that lines the path to the center of the chamber, then hurl it at the transparisteel case. Your roll# + your strength# + 1 is your adventure#.

If your adventure# is equal to or more than 7, add the difference + 10 to your AP total. The hurled stone shatters the brittle transparisteel case, leaving you with open access to the green power gem. You remove the gem from the pedestal, and you may proceed.

If your adventure# is less than 7, subtract the difference from your AP total. The hurled stone bounces off the transparisteel case. Despite its age, the case is still quite strong. Proceed to either use a weapon (below) or, if you have not already tried it, twist the case's dial (above).

To use a weapon: Choose your weapon. Roll the 20-dice to aim at the transparisteel case. Your roll# + your weaponry# + your weapon's close-range# is your adventure#.

If your adventure# is equal to or more than 15, add the difference + 10 to your AP total. Using your weapon, you create a wide hole in the side of the transparisteel case, allowing you to reach into it and remove the green power gem. You may proceed.

If your adventure# is less than 15, subtract 6 from your AP total. Your weapon only created a small hole in the side of the transparisteel case. Employing skill, you must use your weapon as a tool to expand the size of the hole. To make a larger hole, roll the 20-dice again. Your new roll# + your weaponry# + your weapon's close-range# is your new adventure#.

> *If your new adventure# is equal to or more than 15*, add the difference to your AP total. You skillfully use your weapon to expand the hole in the side of the case, allowing you to reach through the hole and remove the green power gem from the pedestal. You may proceed.

> *If your new adventure# is less than 15*, subtract the difference from your AP total. The hole is still not large enough. Go back "To make a larger hole," and repeat. When you have expanded the hole in the case and obtained the green power gem, you may proceed.

You admire the powerful color of the third gem—it looks like a lightsaber ablaze.

You have the third power gem. Add 50 to your AP total.

Standing beside the transparisteel case, you are in the process of placing the green power gem in your backpack when you hear a loud *hum*. Before you can move away from the case, a force field surrounds your position, trapping you in the center of the circular chamber. Outside the force field, the three surrounding insectoid statues remain standing like mute sentinels. You surmise that the force field was installed as additional protection for the green power gem, and that the field was activated when you removed the gem from its pedestal.

You remember the special nature of the power gems, with their auras that can shatter force fields. To escape from the force field, choose to either use the blue power gem, the red power gem, or the green power gem.

To use the blue power gem: Roll the 20-dice to extract the blue power gem from your backpack. Your roll# is your adventure#.

If your adventure# is equal to or more than 11, add the difference + 15 to your AP total. The blue power gem disrupts the force field, allowing you to step away from the center of the circular chamber. You may proceed.

If your adventure# is less than 11, subtract the difference from your AP total. The force field is resistant to the blue gem. Proceed to use the red power gem (below) or the green power gem (below).

To use the red power gem: Roll the 20-dice to extract the red power gem from your backpack. Your roll# is your adventure#.

If your adventure# is equal to or more than 12, add the difference + 20 to your AP total. The red power gem disrupts the force field, allowing you to step away from the center of the circular chamber. You may proceed.

If your adventure# is less than 12, subtract the difference from your AP total. The force field is resistant to the red gem. Proceed to either use the green power gem (below) or, if you have not already tried it, the blue power gem (above).

To use the green power gem: Roll the 20-dice to extract the green power gem from your backpack. Your roll# is your adventure#.

If your adventure# is equal to or more than 10, add the difference + 7 to your AP total. The green power gem disrupts the force field, allowing you to step away from the center of the circular chamber. You may proceed.

If your adventure# is less than 10, subtract the difference from your AP total. Maybe you're holding the green gem the wrong way. Go back and repeat. When you have broken through the force field, you may proceed.

You are returning the power gems to your backpack when you hear something move within the chamber. Turning, you see that the three stone statues of the insectoids appear to be trembling. At first, you think another tremor is responsible, but the statues are the only things shaking in the chamber. To your amazement, all three statues suddenly burst open like exploding shells, revealing the bodies of three insectoids who had been concealed within. Apparently, the "statues" were formfitting containers designed to preserve the three insectoids, and the energy of the nearby force field caused the containers to crumble.

Standing amidst the rubble of their containers, the three insectoids are virtually identical, each with four claw-tipped arms and two multifaceted eyes. One is slightly taller and has a wider head. All three turn to look at you.

The insectoids are alive.

The tallest insectoid's mandibles retract, and it lets out a shrill shriek. You suspect the shriek was a command, since it prompts the two shorter insectoids to raise their claws and lurch toward you.

Before dealing with the tallest insectoid, you must combat the two who are about to sink their claws into you. Choose to either make the two insectoids attack each other (using Power), combat both insectoids at once, or fight one insectoid at a time.

To make the two insectoids attack each other (using Power)*: Choose your Force Movement, Persuasion, or Alteration Power. Roll the 20-dice to make the insectoids turn their claws on each other. Your roll# + your power# + your Power's mid-range# is your adventure#.

If your adventure# is equal to or more than 10, add the difference + 15 to your AP total. The two insectoids are slain by their own claws. You may proceed.

If your adventure# is less than 10, subtract the difference from your AP total. Either you are unable to concentrate or the insectoids are immune to your Power. Proceed to combat both insectoids at once (below).

*NOTE: This counts as one of three Power uses you are allowed on this adventure.

To combat both insectoids at once: Roll the 20-dice to leap between the two insectoids. Your roll# + your stealth# + 3 is your adventure#.

If your adventure# is equal to or more than 15, add the difference + 15 to your AP total. As you leap between the two insectoids, they swing at you but accidentally strike each other with their lethal claws. The two insectoids slay each other, and you may proceed.

If your adventure# is less than 15, subtract the difference from your AP total. You leap between the two insectoids with the hope that they will turn fast and accidentally claw each other, but your effort fails. Proceed to fight one insectoid at a time (below).

To fight one insectoid at a time: Choose your weapon. Roll the 10-dice to aim at an insectoid. Your roll# + your weaponry# + your weapon's mid-range# is your adventure#.

If your adventure# is equal to or more than 15, add the difference + 15 to your AP total. You strike the insectoid, and the menacing creature collapses to the chamber floor. Now that you have defeated the first insectoid, go back "To fight one insectoid at a time," and repeat. When you have defeated both insectoids, you may proceed.

If your adventure# is less than 15, subtract 6 from your AP total. The insectoid evades your attack and moves closer to you. To strike down the insectoid, roll the 10-dice again. Your new roll# + your weaponry# + your weapon's close-range# is your new adventure#.

If your new adventure# is equal to or more than 15, add the difference + 5 to your AP total. Just as the insectoid prepares to rake its claws through you, you use your weapon to vanquish the murderous creature. If one of the two insectoids remains undefeated, go back "To strike down the insectoid," and repeat. When both insectoids have been defeated, you may proceed.

If your new adventure# is less than 15, subtract the difference from your AP total. Considering that the insectoid only just awakened after being in suspended animation for thousands of years, the creature moves surprisingly fast. Go back "To strike down the insectoid," and repeat. After you have defeated both insectoids, you may proceed.

Staring at the two defeated insectoids, the third insectoid shrieks again, then turns to face you. The insectoid's mandibles make a nasty snapping sound, and you think of the hieroglyphics that you saw earlier. You have no doubt that this surviving insectoid wants nothing more than to make a meal of you.

Above the insectoid's head, a heavy stalactite is suspended from the ceiling. Choose to either knock the stalactite from the ceiling, use a weapon to combat the insectoid, or fight the insectoid with your bare hands.

To knock the stalactite from the ceiling: Choose your weapon. Roll the 10-dice to aim at the stalactite. Your roll# + your weaponry# + your weapon's far-range# is your adventure#.

If your adventure# is equal to or more than 9, add the difference + 10 to your AP total. Using your weapon, you cause the stalactite to snap free from the ceiling. The heavy stalactite falls and crushes the insectoid below. You may proceed.

If your adventure# is less than 9, subtract the difference from your AP total. You miss the stalactite, and the insectoid steps aside. The stalactite is no longer directly over the insectoid's head. Proceed to use a weapon to combat the insectoid (below) or fight the insectoid with your bare hands (below).

To use a weapon to combat the insectoid: Choose your weapon. Roll the 20-dice to aim at the insectoid. Your roll# + your weaponry# + your weapon's mid-resist# is your adventure#.

If your adventure# is equal to or more than 15, add the difference + 11 to your AP total. With lethal precision, you cut down the fiendish insectoid. You may proceed.

If your adventure# is less than 15, subtract 6 from your AP total. The insectoid dodges your attack and moves in closer. To re-aim at the insectoid, roll the 20-dice again. Your new roll# + your weaponry# + your weapon's close-resist# is your new adventure#.

If your new adventure# is equal to or more than 15, add the difference to your AP total. This time, you strike the insectoid down. You have defeated all three insectoids, and you may proceed.

If your new adventure# is less than 15, subtract the difference from your AP total. The insectoid knocks your weapon from your grip. Proceed to fight the insectoid with your bare hands (below).

To fight the insectoid with your bare hands: Roll the 20-dice to throw a punch at the insectoid's wide head. If defense is one of your talents, your roll# + your skill# + your strength# is your adventure#. If defense is not one of your talents, your roll# + your strength# is your adventure#.

If your adventure# is equal to or more than 13, add the difference + 12 to your AP total. For all of its ferocity, the insectoid has a surprisingly weak neck. With a single blow, you slay the fiendish insectoid. You may proceed.

If your adventure# is less than 13, subtract 5 from your AP total. The insectoid dodges your punch and nearly slashes you with its razor-sharp claws. You decide to launch a deadly kick to the insectoid's head. To kick the insectoid, roll the 20-dice again for your new roll#. If defense is one of your talents, your new roll# + your skill# + your strength# + 2 is your new adventure#. If defense is not one of your talents, your new roll# + your strength# + 1 is your new adventure#.

If your new adventure# is equal to or more than 13, add the difference + 4 to your AP total. Your powerful kick snaps the insectoid's neck, and the vanquished creature collapses to the chamber floor. You may proceed.

If your new adventure# is less than 13, subtract the difference from your AP total. The insectoid dodges your kick. Go back "To kick the insectoid," and repeat. When you have defeated the insectoid, you may proceed.

You feel a cool draft from the dark passage that leads out of the chamber. The draft suggests the passage may lead directly up to Nallastia's surface. After entering the passage, you walk until the path is interrupted by a deep, wide crevice.

The path continues on the other side of the crevice. You consider jumping over the crevice when you notice a row of stalactites across the passage's ceiling and a ledge that runs along the passage wall. Although a daring jump is not impossible, scaling the ledge or swinging from one stalactite to the next might be safer alternatives.

To continue through the passage, choose to either jump over the crevice, scale the ledge, or swing from the stalactites.

To jump over the crevice: Roll the 20-dice to make a daring jump. If jumping is one of your talents, your roll# + your strength# is your adventure#. If jumping is not one of your talents, your roll# is your adventure#.

If your adventure# is equal to or more than 11, add the difference + 10 to your AP total. You hurtle through the air and land on the other side of the crevice. You may proceed.

If your adventure# is less than 11, subtract the difference from your AP total. Your jump falls short! In midair, you twist your body to land on the ledge that runs along the passage wall. Proceed to scale the ledge (below) or swing from the stalactites (below).

To scale the ledge: Roll the 10-dice to move along the ledge to the other side of the crevice. Your roll# + your stealth# is your adventure#.

If your adventure# is equal to or more than 7, add the difference + 10 to your AP total. Moving carefully along the ledge, you travel over the crevice until you arrive at the other side, where the passage continues. You may proceed.

If your adventure# is less than 7, subtract the difference from your AP total. The ledge crumbles underneath your weight, and you desperately reach out and grab the end of the nearest stalactite. Dangling over the chasm, you realize there is now only one way to continue through the passage. Proceed to swing from the stalactites (below).

To swing from the stalactites: Roll the 20-dice to reach out and grip one stalactite after another until you arrive at the other side of the crevice. Your roll# + your strength# is your adventure#.

If your adventure# is equal to or more than 12, add the difference + 9 to your AP total. Moving like a brachiating simian, you travel hand over hand, gripping each successive stalactite until you cross the crevice. You may proceed.

If your adventure# is less than 12, subtract 5 from your AP total. You are almost at the other side of the crevice when you lose your grip on the last stalactite. Falling, you reach out and catch the upper edge of the crevice. To pull yourself up, roll the 20-dice again. Your new roll# + your strength# + 1 is your new adventure#.

If your new adventure# is equal to or more than 12, add the difference to your AP total. Your fingers dig into the ground as you pull yourself up to safety. You have arrived at the other side of the chasm, and you may proceed.

If your new adventure# is less than 12, subtract the difference from your AP total. You need to pull harder. Go back "To pull yourself up," and repeat. When you have hauled yourself up to the area where the passage continues, you may proceed.

You continue through the passage until you emerge at a small opening that is partially obstructed by overgrown weeds. After pushing your way through the weeds, you are relieved to look up and see the star-lit sky of Nallastia. The air smells fresh.

Incredibly, you are not far from the entrance to the Cavern of Screaming Skulls. You pull your vehicle out from its foliage cover. Proceed to fly back to the fortress.

To fly back to the fortress: Roll the 20-dice to fly fast down the mountain. If navigation is one of your talents, your roll# + your navigation# + your vehicle's speed# + your vehicle's distance# + 1 is your adventure#. If navigation is not one of your talents, your roll# + your navigation# + your vehicle's speed# + your vehicle's distance# is your adventure#.

If your adventure# is equal to or more than 16, add the difference + 7 to your AP total. Racing through the air and over the trees, you travel down the side of Mount Octan until you arrive at the fortress of the Skull Queen. You may proceed.

If your adventure# is less than 16, subtract 5 from your AP total. Flying down the side of Mount Octan, you are nearly at the fortress when a stong gust of wind sends you spiraling across the sky. To regain control of your vehicle, roll the 20-dice again. Your new roll# + navigation# + your skill# + your vehicle's stealth# is your new adventure#.

If your new adventure# is equal to or more than 17, add the difference to your AP total. Expertly maneuvering your vehicle, you bring it under control and arrive at the Skull Queen's fortress. You may proceed.

If your new adventure# is less than 17, subtract the difference from your AP total. Another gust of wind prevents you from regaining control. You need to try again. Go back "To regain control of your vehicle," and repeat. When you have safely arrived at the fortress, you may proceed.

Flying over the Skull Queen's fortress, you steer your vehicle to the Trinity Stones. There, one of your allies stands beside the three megaliths and watches your arrival. Your ally assures you that your other allies—who were stunned by the spider—are recovering well.

The Trinity Stones are now less than two meters from each other, and the forms of Tattyra and Hondu Firewell—still suspended in the force field between the megaliths—remain motionless, apparently unaware of the fact that they are mere minutes away from being crushed to death. Below their floating bodies, the shattered bones of previous victims lie together in a high heap.

You steer your vehicle over the nearest megalith. Reaching into your backpack, you remove the blue power gem and place it on top of the tall standing stone. On the next megalith, you deposit the green power gem, and then you place the red power gem on the final megalith. To your dismay, the force field remains active, and the Trinity Stones continue to converge.

Your ally suggests you rearrange the power gems, as each might be keyed to work with a specific megalith. There are three power gems and three megaliths, giving you six possible combinations. You already know that the combination of blue—green—red does not work, so five possible combinations remain:

blue—red—green

green—red—blue

green—blue—red

red—blue—green

red—green—blue

Now that you know the possible combinations, proceed to rearrange the power gems.

To rearrange the power gems: Roll the 10-dice to place the power gems in their proper order on top of the megaliths. Your roll# is your adventure#.

If you roll 1 or 2, subtract 2 from your AP total. You were about to arrange the stones in the combination of blue-red-green, but you almost drop the final gem. To place the final gem on top of its Trinity Stone, roll the 20-dice for your new roll#.

> *If your new roll# is equal to or more than 11*, add 5 to your AP total. The combination works and you may proceed.

> *If your new roll# is less than 11*, subtract 2 from your AP total. The combination does not work. Go back "To rearrange the power gems," and repeat.

If you roll 3 or 4, Subtract 2 from your AP total. You arrange the stones in the combination of green-red-blue. The combination does not work. Go back "To rearrange the power gems," and repeat.

If you roll 5 or 6, add 5 to your AP total. You arrange the stones in the combination of green-blue-red. The combination works and you may proceed.

If you roll 7 or 8, subtract 2 from your AP total. You arrange the stones in the combination of red-blue-green. The combination does not work. Go back "To rearrange the power gems," and repeat.

If you roll 9 or 0, add 5 to your AP total. You arrange the stones in the combination of red-green-blue. The combination works and you may proceed.

The Trinity Stones stop moving and the force field dissipates. Tattyra and Hondu Firewell's bodies slowly descend to rest on the pile of bones below them. Your ally steps between the megaliths and checks on the Firewells. Their eyes open in surprise. They are unharmed. The last thing they remember is being tossed between the Trinity Stones.

Your ally looks up at you, smiles, and says, "They're all right!"

You have returned from the Cavern of Screaming Skulls with the three power gems known as the Lost Stars of Nallastia. You have brought the gems to the Trinity Stones and saved the Firewells. Add 350 to your AP total.

To read the end of this adventure, please turn to page 97 of your Star Wars Adventures novel, *The Cavern of Screaming Skulls*.